Racetrack Robbery

Ellen Leroe

ILLUSTRATED BY Bill Basso

HYPERION BOOKS FOR CHILDREN
New York

Printed in the United States of America.

First Edition
1 3 5 7 9 10 8 6 4 2

Library of Congress Cataloging-in-Publication Data
Leroe, Ellen, date.
Racetrack Robbery / Ellen Leroe ; illustrated by Bill
Basso. — 1st ed.
p.   cm.
Summary: Artie's invisible pet Ghost Dog helps him solve the case
of the missing lucky coin.
ISBN 0-7868-0093-3 (trade)—ISBN 0-7868-1092-0 (pbk.)
[1. Animal ghosts—Fiction. 2. Dogs—Fiction. 3. Ghosts—
Fiction. 4. Mystery and detective stories.] I. Basso, Bill, ill.
II. Title.
PZ7.L5614Gi   1995
[Fic]—dc20   95-8912

The artwork for each picture is prepared using pencil with ink wash.
This book is set in 13-point Leawood Book.

Once again for Gordon Marks,
my expert consultant on racing!

—E. L.

The trouble began Friday after school at the baseball card meeting. Danny Hockstetter pulled out his National Hot Rod Association drag racing cards and dropped them on top of my latest Whitey Ford and Mickey Mantle finds.

"These are the hottest top-fuel drivers," he boasted. "I've got Eddie Hill, Joe Amato, and Kenny Bernstein, but my favorite is Speed

Bryant. He's so fast he's almost broken the 314-mile-per-hour record."

I tried to get back to talking about baseball and *my* collection, but Danny wouldn't let me. He droned on and on about his top fuel dragster hero until I couldn't take it any longer. That's when I told the fib that would get me into so much trouble over the weekend.

"My dad's taking me to the raceway in Englishtown this weekend," I said, "and he *knows* Speed Bryant. He knows practically all the race car drivers."

That was only partially true. I was going to Englishtown on Sunday for the Autumn Nationals, but my father didn't know anybody. Danny stopped bragging. He shot me a quizzical look.

"Your father knows Speed Bryant, one of the fastest racers in history?"

I felt a warning nudge against my leg under the table and a wet nose against my hand, but I couldn't retract what I had said. Not even when my own dog gave me the signal.

In fact, the fib got even more embellished.

"Oh, sure," I said. "My dad and Speed are friends."

Danny gave me a suspicious-looking smile that made my heart sink. Did he know I was lying? But he didn't say anything, just pulled the Speed Bryant card out of the pack and held it in front of my face.

"Well, that's great," he said, "because I happen to know that Speed's going to be racing his top fuel dragster, the Double Eagle, at Englishtown this weekend. So if your dad's such good friends with him, then you can get him to autograph my card for me."

"Oh," I said in a weak voice. "Well, I don't know."

The eyes of Michael, Todd, and Jamie were glued on me. I was watching Danny. He tossed the Speed Bryant card up in the air and let it fall on the table right in front of me.

"What's not to know, Artie? You just said your father was friends with Speed Bryant. Why can't you get him to sign my card?"

I hesitated, not wanting to confess that I had lied, but knowing I couldn't promise Danny anything.

The tug under the table became stronger, and now I heard a loud, sharp barking. My wrinkly-faced pug was sending me the message to admit the truth, but luckily no one else in Danny's basement got it.

No one got it because no one else heard it. My pug is a poltergeist, an invisible pet I call Ghost Dog. I am the only one who can see Ghost Dog, but he is real, all right. I had met him seven weeks before, on Labor Day. My

family had gone to visit my grandpa Noonie's new house and guess what? The place was haunted—by Ghost Dog! And he mysteriously appeared only to me and my two-year-old sister, Sarah. At first he got me into trouble with my cousins and my mother, but when he helped track down the thief who had stolen my Tom Seaver rookie card, he and I became fast friends.

More than friends, actually. A team. And nine-year-old Aristotle "Artie" Jensen (that's me) and a smart pug with a nose for detection (that's Ghost Dog) had actually solved a mystery on our own and gotten in the papers. No other boy had a pet as special as Ghost Dog. No other boy had a pet as pushy. He didn't like the fact that I was lying to Danny about Speed Bryant, and he was barking up a storm to tell me so. I didn't like the fact, either, but what could I do?

Danny was waiting for my answer with this weird grin on his face. At that moment all I wanted to do was wipe away that smug expression. I picked up the card of super racer Speed Bryant.

"All right," I said. "I'll do it. I'll get his card signed for you."

Danny's mouth dropped open. He stared at me for a few seconds as if I were crazy, then scrambled in his backpack and produced a camera.

"Since you can get an autograph," he said, "why not get a picture, too? I want one of you sitting in Speed's dragster."

He handed me the camera, which I took with trembling fingers. Too late to back down now. I had told a little fib and now I was in a mess.

"I'm really done for," I groaned as my poltergeist pug and I left the meeting and headed for home. "What am I going to do?"

Ghost Dog waddled alongside me and barked noisily. There were no words, but the meaning was clear. I had gotten into trouble because of my big mouth, and it was all my fault.

"I *know* all that," I said, "but can't you think of a way to get Speed Bryant to sign Danny's card and let me photograph his dragster?"

Ghost Dog's short barks turned into growls.

That meant he was thinking about the problem.

If my poltergeist pug put his mind to it, maybe there was hope after all.

2

Saturday afternoon I stayed in my room, pretending to do homework but secretly talking to Ghost Dog. I paced up and down, swinging my baseball bat in the air and executing one pretend home run after another. My wrinkly-nosed pug squatted at the foot of the bed, making faces at my ideas to secure Speed Bryant's autograph.

"Maybe I can get sick," I said, "and that's my excuse for not going to the track and getting Speed's autograph."

Ghost Dog vaulted in the air and made fierce barking noises.

"OK, OK, you want to see Englishtown and so do I," I said in a gloomy voice. "Getting sick is out of the question. So what do you suggest?"

My dog ceased barking and made a funny face at me, the one that told me he didn't have a clue.

"Look," I said, "you've *got* to come up with something, because if you don't, I won't be able to face loudmouth Danny Hockstetter again. And that means no more after-school baseball card meetings."

Ghost Dog wagged his tail dispiritedly. He scrunched up that ugly little mug of his and tried to concentrate. Before he could come up with anything, my baby sister opened the door and poked her head in.

"Hey," I yelled, "you can't come in here!"

Try telling that to a two year old. *No* is Sarah's favorite and most-repeated word. She shouted "No!" with all her might and ran into my room.

"Sarah!" I yelled, and jumped in front of Ghost Dog.

But the Terrible-Two Monster had spotted him before he disappeared.

How could I stop her from shouting out the news and alerting my mother? Ghost Dog is *my* secret and I didn't want Sarah divulging that secret in baby talk. She screamed and I screamed back. Pretty soon we were wrestling on the floor.

"What in the world is going on?" my mother asked, coming in the room with a scowl on her face.

I wrenched my sister off my leg and faced my mom.

"Why, nothing," I said, and gave her my most innocent smile.

"Nothing, my eye. I could hear you two yelling all the way from downstairs, and our company's here for dinner."

"Doggy!" Sarah shouted. She ran around the room, searching under the bed, crawling into the closet. "Where's doggy?"

My mother raised her eyebrows. "Not that pretend pet of yours again? Honestly, Aristotle, you know we can't have a dog in this small space, so stop driving me crazy with your little invisible pet jokes."

"Doggy gone?" Sarah asked. She plopped down and started to cry.

My mom picked her up and frowned at me. "Do you see what you're doing to your little sister? She believes in that pretend pet of yours. Now go get washed up. Mr. Travers and his daughter are here, and dinner's just about ready."

She turned and left the room with my sister. I kicked at an old football on the floor. It bounced against the dresser and knocked down all of my rubber dinosaurs. Grimacing at myself in the mirror, I hurriedly smoothed back my hair and went downstairs.

Mr. Travers is our next door neighbor and a friend of my dad's. He loves drag racing and attends as many events as he can at Englishtown and other local tracks. Tomorrow Mr. Travers would be going with us to Englishtown. Unfortunately, his eight-year-old daughter, Jennifer, would be going, too. Jennifer is bossy and spoiled, and she always tries to tell me what to do. I didn't want her traipsing after me at the racetrack tomorrow. I'd have enough on my hands with trying to get Speed Bryant's autograph.

Jennifer won the brattiness award at dinner, kicking me under the table, making faces. But then Mr. Travers pulled the Speed Bryant card from my hand and I forgot all about his bossy daughter.

"One of the best, and the fastest, in the business. And he's racing tomorrow in the finals."

"Uh, that's great," I said, "but do you happen to know if he ever signs cards?"

Ben Travers threw back his head and laughed. "Speed *never* autographs *anything*—racing cards, programs, nothing. It's a big superstition with him. In fact, he's so superstitious, he won't allow anyone to touch his car except his trusted pit crew."

I swallowed nervously. "But can't someone take a picture of the Double Eagle?"

Mr. Travers scratched his head. "From what I hear, Speed keeps the car so far away from the crowd that no one can get close enough to do that."

My face fell. No picture. No autograph. I was really in trouble now.

3

The raceway in Englishtown was the largest, noisiest place I had ever seen. When we arrived early Sunday afternoon, dragsters were already roaring down the track. Crowds in the stands cheered, whistled, and clapped. It was wall-to-wall people. How would I ever be able to find Speed Bryant's car, let alone take a picture of it?

Suddenly Ghost Dog began barking. He

spotted a big black and silver van heading across the race grounds toward the food stands. DOUBLE EAGLE was painted in large gold letters on the side. Without warning, Ghost Dog took off, chasing after the van.

"Dad," I shouted, "there goes Speed Bryant! Can we go over there to watch him work on his car before the big race?"

My father hesitated. "But we just got here, Artie. Don't you want to watch some other races first?"

"I want to go with Artie," Jennifer whined, and stuck like glue beside me. Ugh.

"I'll stay here and save you good seats," Mr. Travers said with a sigh.

My dad led Jennifer and me across the noisy, crowded grounds. There were trailers, motor homes, stock cars, and top fuel cars all jammed into one small area.

I could hear Ghost Dog barking up a storm,

and I got my dad and Jennifer to head in the same direction. As we approached the food stands I spotted my pug jumping up and down. Directly behind him was Speed Bryant's van and the black, needle-thin Double Eagle. Three crew members were working on the car and had just started barbecuing hot dogs on a small hibachi. They weren't planning on deserting the dragster for a minute, I glumly realized. I'd *never* get an opportunity to get close enough to snap a picture.

"I'm starved," my father said. "Why don't I wait in line and buy us all some lunch while you check out Speed's car?"

Ghost Dog was hungry, too. Before the crew members knew what was happening, my invisible dog raced over and gobbled up every single hot dog on their hibachi!

One of the men turned around. "Hey, what happened to our hot dogs?" he exclaimed.

"If this is your idea of a practical joke, it's not very funny," another snapped.

"I didn't touch them," the third man said, hurling his wrench to the ground. "But I don't care who ate them, I'm going over to the food stands to get some lunch."

All three crew members put their tools down and ambled over to the end of the long line at the food stand. Thanks to Ghost Dog, there was no one near the Double Eagle. Now was the perfect opportunity to photograph Speed's car.

"You and Jennifer come right back here in a few minutes," my father told me. "No wandering off, understand?"

"Yes, sir," I said.

Grumbling under my breath, I led the way to the van. The coast was completely clear and Speed's crew members were too busy looking at the menu to check on the car.

Ghost Dog raced up and down by the Double Eagle, waiting impatiently for me to join him.

I was about to when something unexpected happened.

Speed Bryant popped up from out of nowhere and headed for his van. I recognized the race car driver from Danny's NHRA card. Who could miss that long, bushy red hair and mustache, plus the Speed Bryant cap and Double Eagle warm-up jacket? He glanced over his shoulder before slipping into the van, and I nudged Jennifer to stay out of sight. Seconds later he came back out, stuffing something into a blue canvas bag. He fiddled with something on the steering wheel of his car, then zipped up the canvas bag.

Before I could move, Jennifer grabbed the camera and rushed close to the car. *Click! Click!* In record time, she had snapped two pictures.

Amazingly enough, Speed Bryant didn't yell or order us away from his prized Double Eagle when he spotted Jennifer. He actually waved us over!

"You want a better picture of the car?" he asked. "Let me take one with the both of you in it."

I couldn't believe our good fortune. I of-

fered the camera to Speed Bryant and then scooted over to the car.

Speed Bryant backed away, camera raised to his eye.

Funny, I thought. He was wearing red high-top sneakers. Strange shoes for a big race, but Speed Bryant seemed like a strange man.

"How come you get to sit in front?" Jennifer

demanded when I slid into the front seat.

We started arguing, and then Ghost Dog started barking.

I looked around.

Speed Bryant had disappeared. The top fuel driver had vanished into the crowd, taking Danny's camera with him!

4

I blinked in horrified surprise. For several seconds I couldn't move or speak. Speed Bryant had stolen Danny Hockstetter's camera!

Ghost Dog charged off into the crowd. Then Jennifer did, too.

Both were hot on the trail of the top fuel dragster. What else could go wrong?

I found out ten seconds later as I was

scrambling out of the Double Eagle. A heavy hand fell on my shoulder.

"Just what do you think you're doing in my car?" a voice growled.

I turned to confront a visibly angry Speed Bryant. His ice blue eyes burned into mine.

"You just told me I could sit in it," I blurted. "You even took a picture with my camera."

"What picture? What camera?" he retorted. "I've never seen you before in my life! And I never, *ever*, let anyone near the Double Eagle except my crew."

"Well, but, you just waved us over, you said . . ."

He frowned and quickly examined the steering wheel of the car.

"My Double Eagle coin is gone!" he exclaimed. "I'm getting Security over here fast!" He poked a finger in my face. "And you're not going anywhere until we get this matter straightened out."

"But I didn't take any coin," I protested.

The driver ignored me and called for track security guards on a walkie-talkie. As he was talking, I examined him more closely. His bushy red hair, mustache, cap, and jacket were the same as before, but his voice and his eyes were different. Was I going crazy or were there *two* Speed Bryants?

A track security guard arrived a few minutes later. My father quickly hurried over as well, balancing a tray piled high with hamburgers, fries, and sodas.

"Artie, what's going on over here?" my dad said. "And where's Jennifer?"

"I'll tell you what's going on," Speed Bryant said with a scowl. "This boy here climbed into my car and stole my Double Eagle coin.

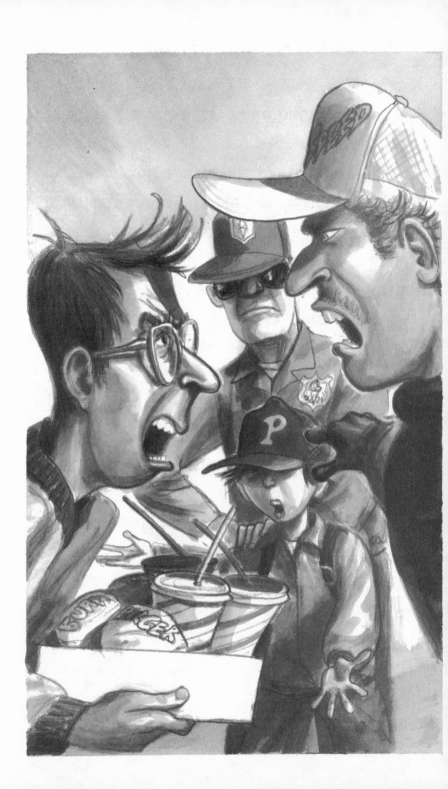

I always keep the twenty-dollar gold piece attached to the steering wheel for luck in a big race, and now he's taken it."

"Dad, I didn't," I burst out. "I did sit in his car, but Speed Bryant, or a man who dressed and looked just like him, told me I could."

Three pairs of eyebrows shot up: the top fuel driver's, the security guard's, and my dad's.

"A man who looked like me?" Speed Bryant demanded. "Now you know the boy's lying. Making up stories like that."

"Now just a minute," my father interrupted. He placed the tray on the ground and faced the guard and Speed Bryant.

"My son doesn't steal. If he says he didn't take this gold coin, then I believe him."

I shoved my backpack at my father. "I didn't, Dad. You can check my backpack, check my jacket and all my pockets. There really was a guy here who told me he was Speed Bryant. He went into the van and then he fooled around with the steering wheel of the car. I saw him do it, and so did Jennifer! And she even took a picture of him with Danny's camera, but he tricked us into handing over the camera and then he took off with it!"

I opened my backpack and deposited the contents on the ground. I did the same with my jacket and pants pockets. While the guard examined all my junk, I explained to my dad about Jennifer running after the phony Speed Bryant.

As if things weren't bad enough, the three crew members returned and discovered that some extra cash had been taken from the van.

"See!" I exclaimed. "That other Speed Bryant stole it! And he took the gold coin!"

The guard looked up from the contents of

my backpack. "Well, there's no Double Eagle coin in the boy's possession."

"Maybe the girl took it, the one he claims ran after the phony me," Speed Bryant said.

"Why won't you believe me?" I shouted. "We've got to find Jennifer. She'll tell you I'm not making any of this up!"

My dad agreed. He requested that Security help in searching for Jennifer, but then Jennifer herself ran right back to the car. I had never been so happy to see Her Brattiness in all my life.

When Jennifer caught sight of Speed Bryant, her mouth flopped open like a fish. She pointed a shaky finger at him.

"But I just saw you disappear!" she said.

5

Everyone turned to stare at her in disbelief.

Speed Bryant nudged the track guard. "What did I tell you, more made-up stories."

"It's not made-up," Jennifer exclaimed. "I ran after you and then you disappeared right before my eyes."

Speed Bryant glowered at the two of us. "I've got a mysterious double who steals my good luck coin, and then the mysterious double disappears right in front of a racetrack full of witnesses. How can anyone believe a word these two kids are saying?"

Everyone began talking at once.

Jennifer pulled me aside.

"What happened, Artie? Why are we in trouble?"

I jammed my Phillies baseball cap down over my eyes.

"You wouldn't believe it," I muttered, and then told Jennifer exactly what happened after she chased the phony Speed Bryant into the crowd.

"You mean the Speed Bryant we saw wasn't really Speed Bryant at all?" Jennifer asked. "And he stole the camera *and* the Double Eagle coin? That's so unbelievable!"

I nodded. "About as unbelievable as your own little magic story."

Jennifer stamped her foot. "I swear it happened! I ran after Speed Bryant—well, the guy we thought was Speed Bryant—following his red hair and white cap, and poof! The red hair and cap disappeared."

"That's impossible," I said, "unless . . ."

I stared at her, beginning to get an idea. What if the first Speed Bryant had been wearing a wig and mustache as a disguise? "Listen," I said, but was interrupted by the track announcer making the first call for Speed's big race.

But Speed Bryant was not ready.

The top fuel driver paced nervously up and down, running a trembling hand through his bushy red hair.

"There's no way I'm going to race without my Double Eagle coin," he moaned. "That gold piece always helps me win!"

"We have to tow the car to the starting

line," one of the crew members said.

"I'm not going anywhere until I get the truth out of these two kids!" Speed Bryant snapped.

Not too far away I heard a familiar sound. Ghost Dog was barking loudly. Did that mean he had located the imposter Speed Bryant?

I had to go to him.

Taking a deep breath, I dodged around the security guard and took off across the grounds. I sprinted in the direction of the barking.

I heard people chasing me, but I didn't stop. I had to find out if Ghost Dog was hot on the trail of the imposter thief.

A crowd was gathering some distance from the food stands. People were laughing and shouting and pointing at something in the middle of a big circle. I heard a man yelling angrily. Above all the noise I heard Ghost Dog barking. He was right in the middle of what-ever was happening.

I pushed my way through the crowd and then stopped short. A dark-haired man in a plaid shirt was chasing after a canvas bag that mysteriously kept jumping out of his reach.

"What's he got in that bag, some kind of animal?" someone asked.

An animal was making the canvas bag move, all right, but an animal only I could see. Ghost Dog kept tugging the bag just out of the owner's reach.

As soon as my dog spotted me, he raced over and dropped the bag at my feet. I picked it up.

"Give me that bag!" the irritated owner shouted.

Red-faced and sweating, the man yanked the bag out of my hands with such force that

it fell. The contents spilled out on the grass. I bent to help the man replace his things when I spotted something familiar.

"That's Danny Hockstetter's camera!" I yelled.

6

The man squinted at me.

"That's Danny's camera," I said, pointing to it.

The man shook his head. "Lots of people own cameras like this. It's a popular model."

He thrust the camera back inside the bag along with the few other spilled items.

"But I know it's my friend's camera," I insisted. "I'm sure it is."

"Well, I'm sure it's my camera, case closed," the man said. He gave me a grin that I didn't trust.

I hesitated, not sure what to do. Could it be possible he was telling the truth and Ghost Dog had tracked down the wrong guy? This dark-haired man certainly didn't look like the person who had claimed he was Speed Bryant.

I stared at him, fidgeting. The crowd whispered and began breaking up. They believed the camera belonged to him, too.

The man shrugged and turned to walk away. Beside me Ghost Dog was jumping up and down and growling.

I scrutinized the man and then something clicked.

He was wearing unusual shoes.

"Red high-tops!" I shouted. "You're the thief who stole the gold coin!"

The man froze, then began walking a little faster.

"After him, Ghost Dog!"

Ghost Dog took off with a flying leap and disappeared into the crowd. Before I could follow him, someone grabbed my arm.

"Not so fast," the track guard said, panting. A frowning Speed Bryant stood right behind him.

"He's getting away!" I shouted, and pointed at the fleeing man.

"Hey, wait a minute, I think I recognize that man," Speed Bryant said.

"Don't let him get away," I pleaded with the guard. "I saw the camera in his bag."

The guard nodded and then the three of us scrambled across the grounds.

"Aristotle, wait up!" my dad shouted behind me, but I couldn't stop. No way would the thief escape this time.

I had him in sight for a while, but then he darted behind a row of motor homes. The guard and Speed and I stopped where we lost him and looked all over. Rows of stock cars, pit crews, and trailers lined the area. The creep had vanished.

"We lost him," the guard declared with a groan.

"No, wait." I tilted my head, straining to hear Ghost Dog. At first I heard nothing, not a peep, but then very faintly I could make out the sound of his bark. It seemed to be coming from the vicinity of the parking lot.

"I think I spotted him!" I lied. "Follow me."

We elbowed past clusters of people, some sitting in deck chairs on the grass, others strolling to the stands. Soon we came to an area with a large stage where musicians were tuning up instruments while a growing audience waited below. Huge amplifiers and drums blocked the back of the stage but I managed to spot Ghost Dog. He was racing crazily around one particularly giant amplifier.

The three of us came to a sudden stop in front of the stage.

"You managed to see the thief in this mob scene?" the guard asked me suspiciously.

"Yeah, well, I did," I said.

What was Ghost Dog trying to tell me? Were all the musicians up there really part of the band? There was no sign of the dark-haired man.

I watched Ghost Dog circling the giant amp and then I saw it.

The tip of a red high-top stuck out just behind the big speaker.

"There!" I shouted, pointing. "He's up on the stage!"

A frightened face peered out from its hiding

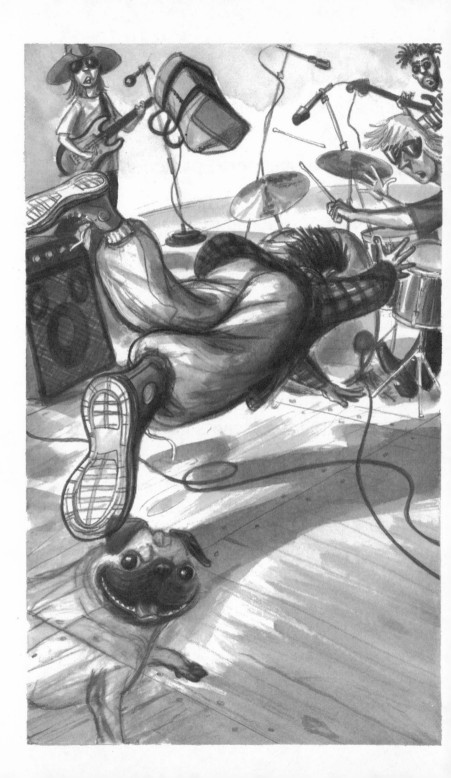

spot and saw us coming. The thief turned to run, canvas bag in hand, but Ghost Dog pounced at his pants leg. The man threw up his arms and stumbled, falling heavily against the set of drums. Down came everything with an explosive crash.

The canvas bag literally flew into my arms as the guard and Speed Bryant tackled the man. I stumbled, too, and Ghost Dog sailed off the stage and landed at my feet.

Then my father and Jennifer came huffing and puffing to the crowded stage.

Talk about a bang-up finish to a chase scene!

But there were more surprises to come when Speed Bryant got a good look at the thief.

7

"I can't believe this!" Speed Bryant exclaimed. "This man is Rod Novack. He used to be a member of my pit crew."

The man twisted and struggled in the track guard's grip.

"Until you fired me," he said, and glared at Speed Bryant.

"I had to," the top fuel driver said. "You were caught stealing money and expensive auto parts from the Double Eagle." He eyed the canvas bag in my arms. "And if we find what I think we'll find in that bag, then you're still up to your old tricks."

My dad pushed forward.

"Aristotle, what's going on? Why did you run off like that?" He raised his eyebrows. "I'm waiting for an explanation, Artie."

Jennifer rushed over to me, eyes gleaming triumphantly.

"Open up the bag," she said. "The camera's probably in there."

I looked over at Rod Novack. "I know it is. I saw it."

"Forget the camera," Speed Bryant snapped. "I want my Double Eagle coin." He seized the bag from my hands and began removing its contents.

"There's Danny's camera!" I shouted gleefully. "See, I told you he took it!"

Without wasting another minute, I grabbed

the stolen object and stashed it in the safety of my backpack.

"And here's the cash from the van," Speed Bryant said, producing a rubber-banded roll of money. Then he fished out objects that made everyone stare—a bushy red wig and phony mustache.

"That's part of his disguise," I explained. "That's why I thought he was you when I first saw him by the car. His cap and jacket should be in there, too."

Sure enough, the Speed Bryant cap and Double Eagle jacket appeared next.

Jennifer snapped her fingers. "He didn't really disappear, then. When he had gotten far enough in front of me, he just pulled off his cap and wig, and bingo! No more Speed Bryant."

"Very clever," the real Speed Bryant said to Rod Novack. "But why go to all this trouble for a lousy seventy-five dollars cash and a twenty-dollar gold piece?"

Rod Novack grinned smugly. "Revenge," he stated. "You ruined my chances of ever working at the racetrack again."

"We've got to find my good luck coin," Speed Bryant exclaimed. He pawed frantically through the remaining contents of the bag. "Where is it?"

Rod Novack laughed. "You won't find it. And I know you can't race without it."

The Englishtown announcer made the final call over the loudspeaker for Speed's big race.

"Final call," Speed Bryant groaned. "We've got to tow the Double Eagle to the starting line or I'm disqualified." He pleaded with the guard. "Search him! I know that coin's got to be on him! He wouldn't just throw it away!"

But it was nowhere to be found.

It wasn't in Rod Novack's clothes or anywhere in the bag.

"I'll lose," Speed Bryant said. "I've never won a race without that coin."

Visibly shaken, the top fuel driver hurried back to his crew and car. The security guard started to lead Rod Novack away.

"Have we had enough excitement for one day?" my father asked wearily.

But there was more to come.

Without warning, Ghost Dog took off after the guard and jumped in front of him. The guard tripped over Ghost Dog and stumbled against Rod Novack. Both men lost their balance and fell down in a heap of arms and legs.

Quick as a flash Ghost Dog sniffed around the guard's jacket, then stuck his face inside the pocket. When Ghost Dog came out, he had a shiny gold coin stuck to the tip of his wet black nose!

8

Ghost Dog had located Speed Bryant's Double Eagle coin!

Rod Novack must have planted it on the guard right after he had been caught and figured no one would think to search the guard's pockets. He was right.

No one had—except for Ghost Dog.

I raced over and pried the coin away from my invisible pet.

"Hey!" I yelled, holding up the coin. "Look what fell out of the guard's jacket!"

The guard yanked Rod Novack to his feet and stared at him.

"Thought you'd hide the Double Eagle on me so no one would find it until well after the big race today? Well, you're out of luck, Novack."

Everyone had a colossal smile on their face.

Everyone, that is, except for Rod Novack. He practically ground his teeth together in anger as the guard dragged him away.

Meanwhile Speed Bryant's race was almost ready to begin.

Would we be able to get the coin to him in time?

My father, Jennifer, Ghost Dog, and I hurried over to the starting line. Mr. Travers called to us from his seat in the stands but we did not have time to answer him. The crew had almost towed Speed Bryant to the staging lanes, an area off-limits to us. Once Speed Bryant was inside those lanes, we wouldn't be allowed to get anywhere near the car.

We had only seconds to spare.

Screaming and waving our hands frantically, we ran up to the staging lanes. Luckily Speed Bryant heard us shouting his name. He turned and I held up the Double Eagle coin.

A smile as bright as a camera flash illuminated his face. He held out his gloved hand.

"Toss it to me!"

Just as the car turned off the staging lanes, I threw the coin at him like Willie McGee launching the ball from left field to second base. Then I swallowed nervously.

It wasn't going to make it.

He was moving away too rapidly.

But Ghost Dog made an awesome leap. He caught the coin in midair and ran alongside the car. He jumped up and wriggled the coin into Speed's outstretched glove.

But then Ghost Dog toppled inside the top fuel car along with the coin! Like the sound of thunder, the engine of the Double Eagle roared to life.

Ghost Dog was trapped!

"Ghost Dog!" I shouted.

Of course, he didn't hear me.

The lights at the starting line flashed green. The Double Eagle charged down the track in an almost magical burst of speed, easily beating out the other racers.

"Bryant's just shattered the 314-mile-per-hour record!" the public address announcer shouted. "This is a real first today!"

I didn't care about that. I cared about my dog. What had happened to him? And then I

spotted him. Speed Bryant had released a back parachute to slow the top fuel car down. Bouncing up and down helplessly in the folds of the parachute was Ghost Dog! He did a few somersaults high in the air, then jumped down on the track. I whistled and he came charging over to me.

Everyone in the stands stood and cheered as Speed's car was towed back to the starting line. I cheered because my hero pug was back at my side. Photographers and TV people pushed in around the beaming driver to take pictures. Even Mr. Travers hurried down from the stands to join in the excitement.

Then Speed Bryant's crew located me in the bottom of the stands.

"Hey, kid, Speed wants you to join him," they said.

I hesitated, but Speed Bryant called out my name and motioned me over. The winning race car driver put his arm around me and waved at the press.

"Here's the newest member of the crew that helped me break my record today," Speed Bryant announced. "His name is Artie."

Flashbulbs exploded in my face as I stood next to Speed. I blinked and Ghost Dog howled.

Speed Bryant leaned down. "You saved the day by finding that Double Eagle coin for me. So if there's anything you want, just say the word."

I hurriedly fished Danny's NHRA card out of my backpack.

"Would you sign a race card?"

"No problem," Speed said, reaching for a pen. "I'll even throw in a racing cap and official crew jacket." He signed his name and then looked at me. "In fact, you deserve to ride with me to the winner's circle. I want you to be there when I get my trophy."

Wait until Danny Hockstetter heard about this!

Speed Bryant lifted me into the race car and Ghost Dog jumped in right next to me.

"You're the *real* winner," I whispered to my hero pug. "And I'm going to reward you with the biggest, juiciest hamburger I can find after all this is over."

Ghost Dog barked happily and licked my face.

This was one race we would never forget!